The Biggest Valentine Ever

by Steven Kroll

Illustrated by Jeni Bassett

SCHOLASTIC INC.

New York Toronto London Auckland Sydney
Mexico City New Delhi Hong Kong Buenos Aires

For Kathleen
— *S. K.*

For Nathan
— *J. B.*

Text copyright © 2006 by Steven Kroll.
Illustrations copyright © 2006 by Jeni Bassett Leemis.
All rights reserved. Published by Scholastic Inc.
SCHOLASTIC, CARTWHEEL BOOKS, and associated logos
are trademarks and/or registered trademarks of Scholastic Inc.

Kroll, Steven.
The biggest valentine ever / by Steven Kroll ; illustrated by Jeni Bassett.   p. cm.
"Cartwheel books."   Summary: When Desmond and Clayton, two mice, finally
learn to cooperate, they create a wonderful valentine for their teacher.
ISBN 0-439-76419-X (pbk.)
[1. Interpersonal relations--Fiction. 2. Valentine's Day--Fiction. 3. Mice--Fiction.]
I. Bassett, Jeni, ill. II. Title.
PZ7.K9225Blg 2006   [E]--dc22   2005009809

10 9 8 7 6 5 4   6 7 8 9/10

Printed in the U.S.A • First printing, January 2006

Once there were two mice who fell in love with
the same valentine, but it didn't start out that way.

The day before Valentine's Day, Mrs. Mousely asked all the students in her class at Mouseville School to make valentine cards. The two friends, Clayton and Desmond, decided to make a card together and give it to Mrs. Mousely as a surprise.

Clayton cut a big heart out of cardboard. Desmond made a heart-shaped hole in the middle.

Desmond cut out some small pink hearts and pasted them around the hole. Then he added a few more.

Clayton glued glitter on the hearts. Then he glued on more glitter. He stepped back.

"You put too many hearts on!" Clayton said.

Desmond was upset. "You put too much glitter on the hearts!"

"Well, why did you make that hole in the middle?" asked Clayton.
"I thought it looked nice," said Desmond.

"It doesn't look nice. It looks awful!" yelled Clayton.
"I think it looks very nice," said Desmond, frowning.
They glared at each other.

"I don't want to make a valentine with you!" yelled Clayton.

"I don't want to make a valentine with you!" yelled Desmond.

They tore their valentine in half.
"I'm going to make my own valentine," said Clayton.
"I'm going to make my own valentine," said Desmond.

That night at dinner, Clayton's dad said, "Son, you look sad. Can I help?"

Clayton hung his head. He told his dad about the valentine.

Clayton's dad thought for a moment. "You guys may make nice valentines on your own, but I think you would make a nicer valentine together."

At that same time, over at Desmond's house,
Uncle Vernon said exactly the same thing.

But Clayton didn't listen to his dad. He marched back
to his room and began to make his very own valentine.

He cut a big heart out of cardboard, but he didn't put a hole in the middle. He put pink hearts around the edge, but not enough pink hearts.

Then Clayton put glitter on the hearts, but it was too much glitter. He stepped back and looked at his valentine. It just wasn't right.

At the same time, Desmond was making his very own valentine.
He cut a big heart out of cardboard, but he wasn't good at cutting
large things and the heart was lopsided.

He made a neat, heart-shaped hole in the middle, but then he put too many hearts around the hole. He sprinkled on some glitter, but not enough glitter.

Desmond stepped back and looked at his valentine. It just wasn't right.

The next morning, Clayton and Desmond took the school bus. They sat far away from each other. But as they were getting off, Desmond tripped on the stairs. He bumped into Clayton, and they fell down.

"I think we should try making our valentine again," said Clayton.
"No one said we couldn't," said Desmond.

In art class, Clayton and Desmond put their heads together and came up with a plan.

Then Clayton cut out the biggest, most perfect red heart anyone had ever seen. They added a pink heart to fit in the middle.

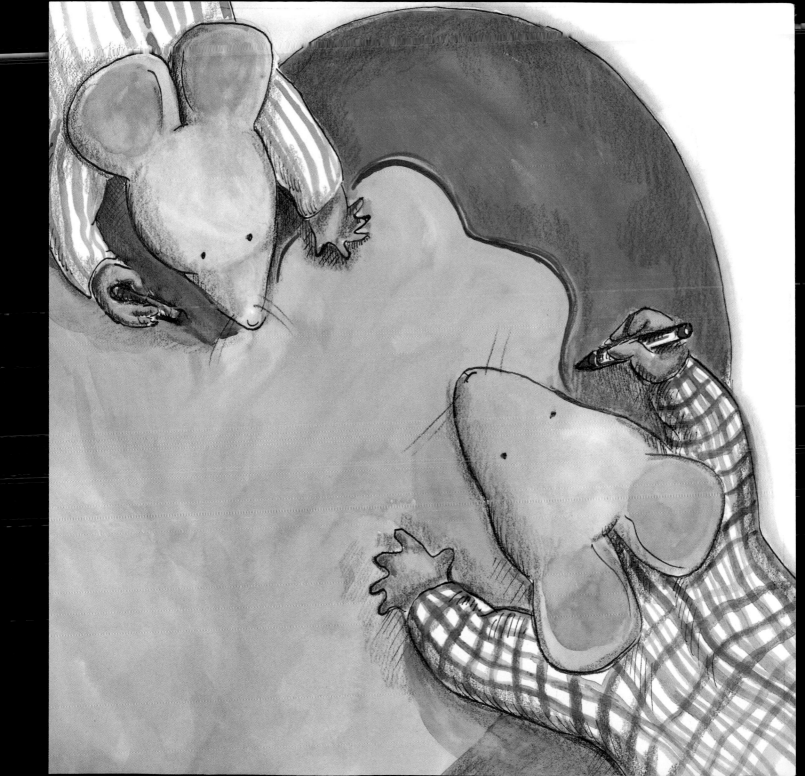

Then Desmond, who was good at cutting small things, cut out some tiny pink hearts and pasted them onto the big red heart.

Clayton added some glitter and cut out a bunch of other hearts.

Desmond made a nose on one—
and a mischievous eye.

Then they glued all the hearts together.

They stepped back to look at their card.
It was a giant valentine mouse!

"Wow!" said Clayton. "We did it!"
"Wow!" said Desmond. "We did it together!"
They gave each other a high five.

They cut up a lace doily and glued it around the edge.

Then they wrote on their card in big letters:

HAPPY VALENTINE'S DAY
TO MRS. MOUSELY.
WE LOVE YOU.
CLAYTON AND DESMOND.

They carried the valentine to their classroom and gave it to
Mrs. Mousely. She clapped with delight. The whole class cheered.
It was the biggest valentine ever, and it was also the best.